Crayola

My Big Coloring Book

BuzzPop

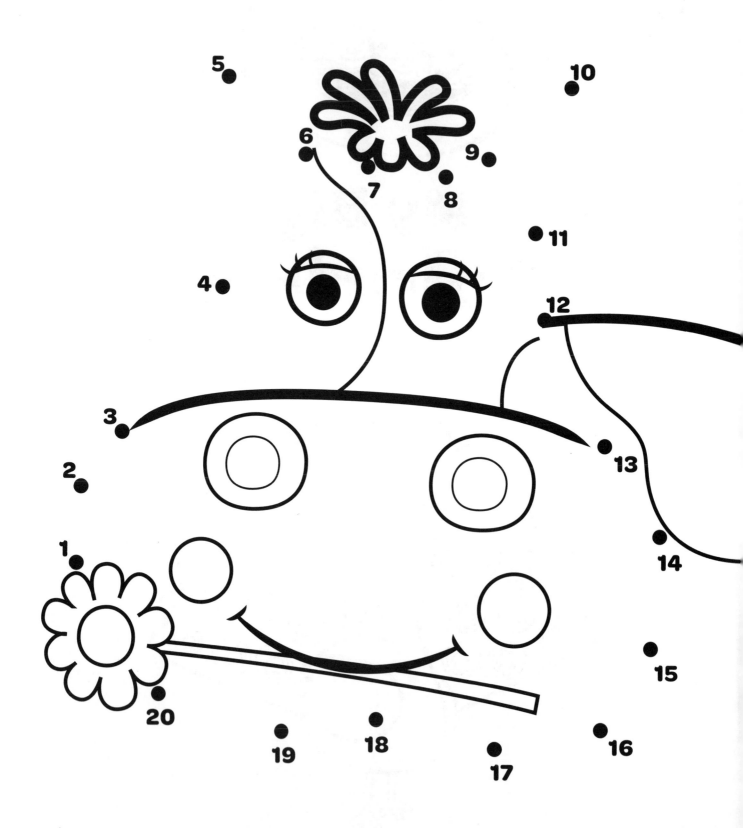

Connect the dots to see who lives on a farm and says "Moo."

How many carrots can this bunny eat?

This fox lives in an enchanted forest.

The snake uses his tongue to smell.

A mermaid castle sits at the bottom of the sea.

Mermaids like to swim. How about you?

What a pretty butterfly.

A walrus soaks up the sun.

**This octopus is waving to you
with all of her arms.**

These magic gumballs can make rain go away.

This panda munches on bamboo.

**The little puppy explores the yard.
What does he find?**

Color this seahorse in bright colors.

What a cute little lion cub.

A

1. Giraffe

B

2. Rhino

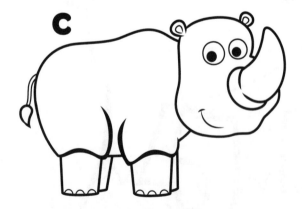

C

3. Lion

Can you match each animal to his name?

Look who is ready to play!

Want to be a superhero today?

Look out! This dragon is hot stuff!

This seal has lots of spots.

Can you use a different color on each stripe on this tiger's tail?

A monkey swings from a vine.

A starfish is shaped like a star.

This rhino has a large horn.

This kind fairy grants wishes to animals.

**The narwhal is a whale with
a tusk on her head.**

This little crab has big claws.

**Can you decorate this castle
for a seashell fairy?**

Look at what is at the bottom of the ocean.

The superhero saves the day!

The elephant sprays water with her trunk.

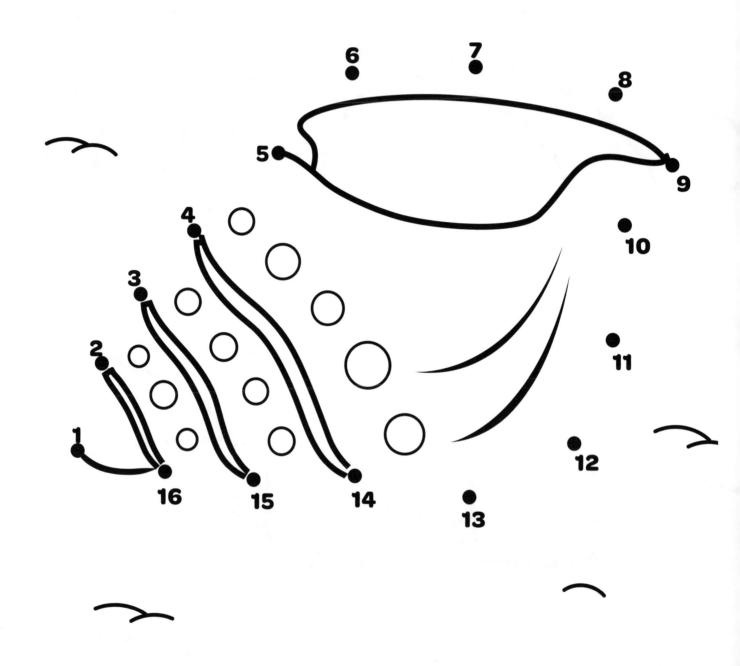

Connect the dots to see a pretty shell from the ocean.

A

B   **C**

Find and circle the hippo that is different from the others. Then color them all.

**Remember to make a wish before
you blow out the candles!**

Let's pretend to be Robin Hood!

The elephant uses his trunk to drink.

This dragon wants a new friend.

A yellow dress with silver sparkles, please!

Here's a sloth, looking around.

Look, it's a baby seal!

Add some silly spots to this zebra.

What color castle would a princess like?

The royal cat and royal mouse play outside.

The prince wears a fancy cloak.

Draw some apples for the giant to pick.

Let's dance and celebrate!

This hippo likes to splish and splash.

Look! The pirate found a magic diamond!

This manatee has found some plants to eat.

This silly monkey takes a picture of himself.

**A ladybug and a butterfly say
hello to each other.**

The panda family is happy to see you.

**A tiny fairy lives inside this tiny house.
Draw her.**

The puppy is ready to play.

This llama wants to find some grass to eat.

Isn't this sea otter cute?

A mother zebra watches over her baby.

This new ballerina can point her toes.

What is your favorite kind of sparkle?

This little tree elf loves the color green.

This lemur is holding her tail.

Koalas spend a lot of time in trees.

Meow! Who left a gift for the kitty?

**Don't these friends look happy
to see each other?**

Color this mongoose's body to match his tail.

**Color the giraffe and zebra and
give them their patterns.**

These lions are happy together.

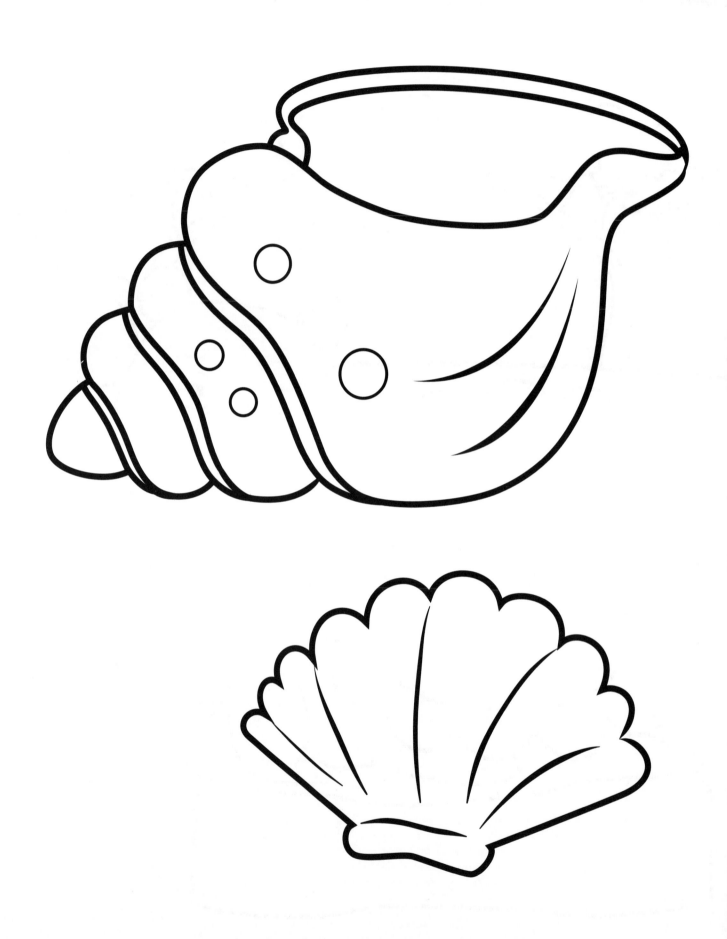

Use pretty colors on these shells.

A wild boar has two tusks.

This monkey likes to hang out.

This robot is saying hello!

Make each butterfly a different color.

Two ocean friends want you to color them.

The ballerina twirls in her tutu.

Say hello to the baby hippo.

A tiny elf sits upon an enchanted mushroom.

Color this crab to look silly.

Ninja warrior!

This frog looks ready to hop.

What a beautiful butterfly.

How many colors can you make this bird?

Sweet treat!

A tortoise walks slowly.

**Who says "Quack"?
Connect the dots to find out.**

An elephant is sturdy on his feet.

**The eagle ray fish glides
to the bottom of the ocean.**

Three fish meet in the ocean.

The king and his court live in a castle.

This frog is a good swimmer.

Can you give this fairy rainbow wings?

You never know who you'll meet.

This crab looks happy on his little island.

**A zebra is black and white,
but this one can be any colors you like.**

Make these animals different colors.

A butterfly spreads her wings.

Jellyfish are found in every ocean.

This girl is ready for a boat ride.

A baby giraffe is six feet tall when she's born.

The genie is giving out wishes!

Every birthday is magical.

What colors do you want this fish's stripes to be?

The princess curtsies and says, "Hello."

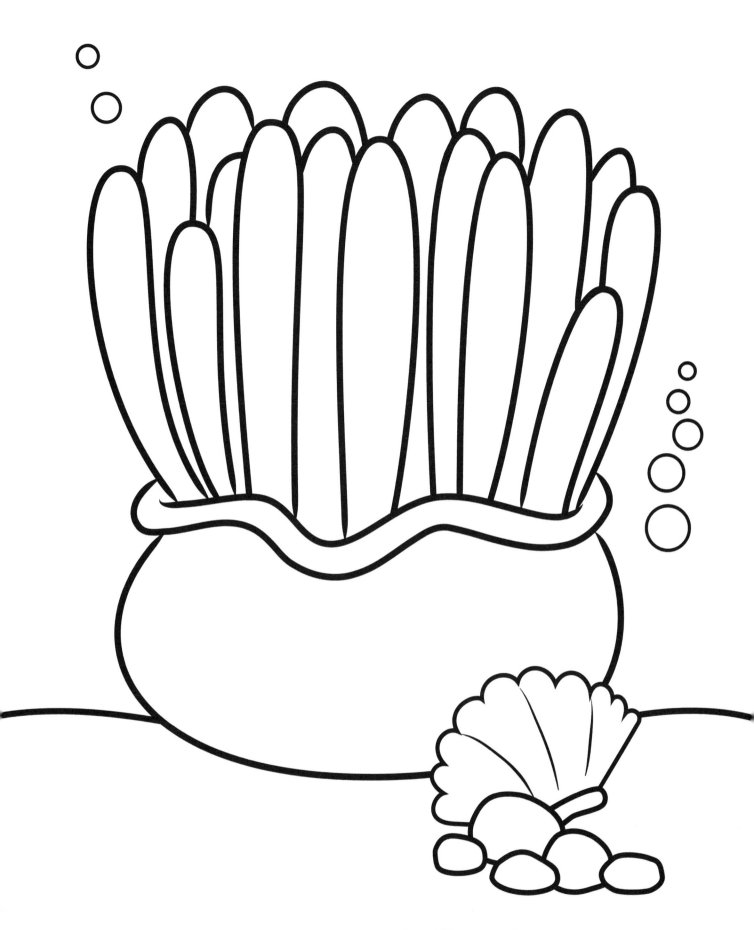

**The sea anemone looks like a plant,
but it is an animal.**

This monkey wants to give you a banana.

Uh-oh! There's a dragon on the castle.

Shh! Two leopards are napping.

What does a princess wear in the summertime?

This fairy is as small as a flower!

Time to cast a spell!

A male lion has a mane.

Let's catch some waves!

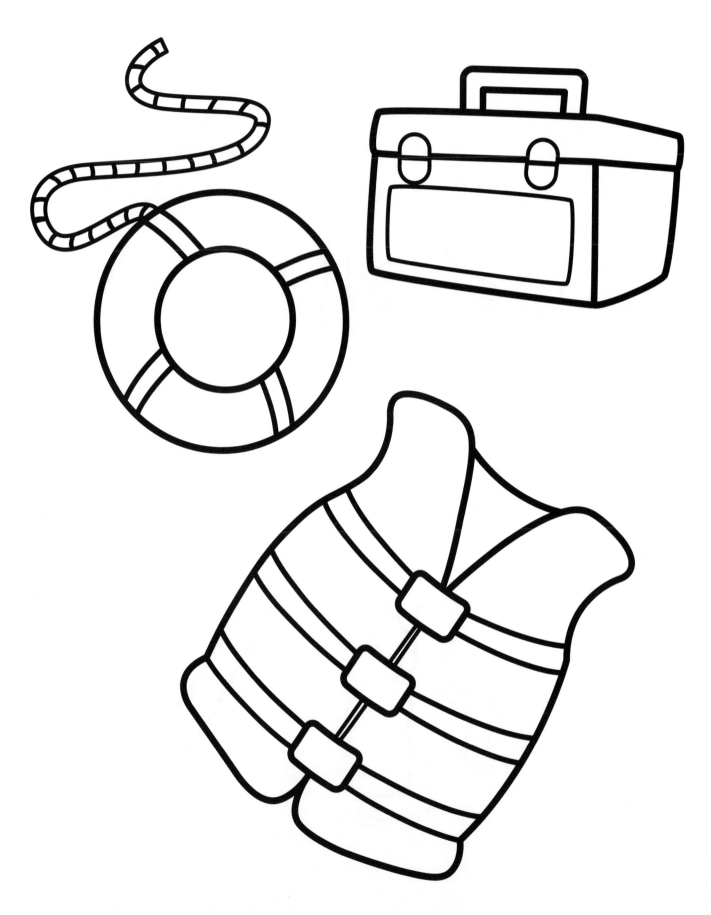

Color these things you need for a boat ride.

This lighthouse's light is shining.

Here's a whale waving her tail.

There is so much to see in the ocean.

What a whale!

Give this puffin a colorful beak.

A flamingo has long legs.

The sun shines on this pretty house.

**Some people say there is treasure
at the bottom of the ocean.**

**Would you like to take a boat ride?
Decorate your boat!**

Blue whales are the world's largest animals.

This shark is called a hammerhead because of the shape of his head.

The unicorn gallops and plays.

A martian has landed!

Two fluttering butterflies.

This parrot lives in the jungle.

Take me to your leader!

The king and queen live in a beautiful castle!

What color is this fuzzy monster's fur?

The Pegasus prances above the clouds.

Surf's up!

Look what has washed up onshore.

This fish is looking right at you!

A lion cub tries to catch a butterfly.

A peacock shows his feathers.

Zoom! **Who is coming to visit?**

Would you like to ride in a submarine?

A turtle's body is covered with a hard shell.

Some fish like to swim together.

Seahorses aren't horses, they're fish!

Next stop? Home!

**An ice cream fairy lives
inside this yummy home.**

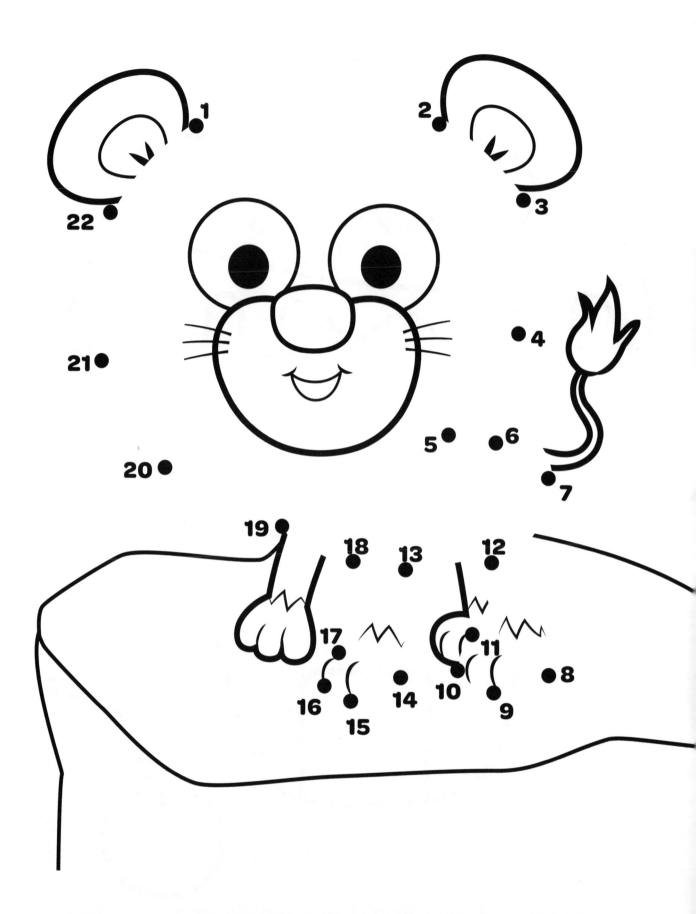

**Connect the dots to see a jungle baby that is
learning how to roar.**

Your answer:

Buzz! How many bees can you count?

Answer: 6

A parrot and a bee both have wings.

This little cub wants you to color him.

An ant can carry many times her body weight.

A snake moves without arms or legs!

What a pretty fish.

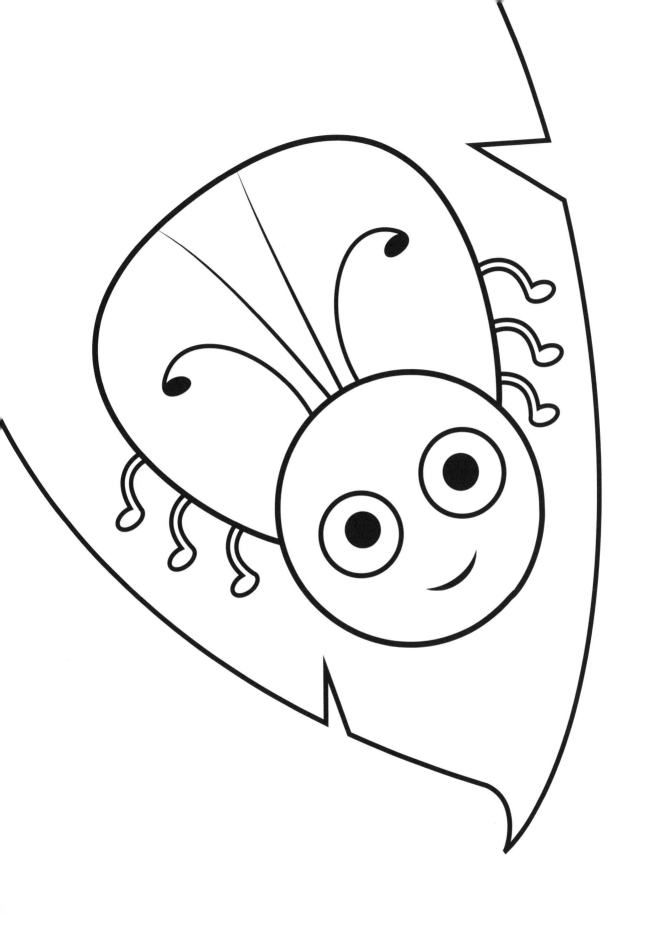

An insect has six legs.

A whale comes up for air.

Sailing the seven seas.

Here is one gorilla with three bananas.

Look at this bird's fancy tail feathers.

Give this squid color and more spots.

A narwhal and a shark swim past each other.

This lizard is ready to take a nap.

This seagull landed on a post.

A seagull rests in her nest.

Make each starfish a different color.

This hippo wants to play.

This bird has just landed on the ground.

Even teddy bears like surprises.

A rocket zooms through outer space!

Your answer:

**Which path will lead the
squirrel to more acorns?**

Answer:2

Have you ever built a sandcastle?

A parrot enjoys the hot, sunny day.

A tiger on the prowl.

Say hello to the penguin.

Animals gather at the river.

Which cupcake would you eat first?

A parrot fish's mouth looks a lot like a beak.

The hermit crab has a beautiful shell.

**Wave to the lizard—
and stick out your tongue, too!**

Your answer:

How many butterflies can you count?

How many different colors can you make these garden flowers?

Clown fish have stripes.

Are you ready to dig for more seashells?

Color this insect in bright colors.

Monkeys love bananas.

Fly, Pegasus, fly!

Who is inside the magic carriage?

"Squawk!" says the parrot.

A bird watches the eggs in her nest.

You can see faraway things with binoculars.

Bats wake up at night.

What colors should this dolphin be?

A fairy flutters her wings to fly.

Doesn't this lion look like he's smiling?

Use your favorite colors on this sailboat.

A puffer fish puffs up when he's scared.

What colors do you want this shark to be?

One royal sundae, coming right up!

Strawberry shortcake! Yum!

This turtle swims toward a large shell.

Color this striped bee.

Two flamingos stand tall.

A bat is flying in the night sky.

It's a horse, of course!

Find and circle the horse that is different from the rest. Then color them all.

A frog flicks his tongue.

"Ribbit, ribbit!" say the jumping frogs.

A polar bear walks onto the frozen ocean.

How colorful can you make this fish?

What a beautiful shell!

This wiggly alien has an eye for adventure!

A mother and baby dolphin swim together.

**Different animals meet at the bottom
of the ocean.**

A dolphin jumps up to say hello to you.

Color this fish and give her some spots.

A clown fish can live in a sea anemone.

**This is a jellyfish.
Color him however you wish.**

A hippo cools off in the water.

This robot is programmed to dance!

Rabbits love carrots.

**"Cock-a-doodle-doo!" the rooster crows
every morning on the farm.**

A leopard has lots of spots.

Look how high this whale has jumped.

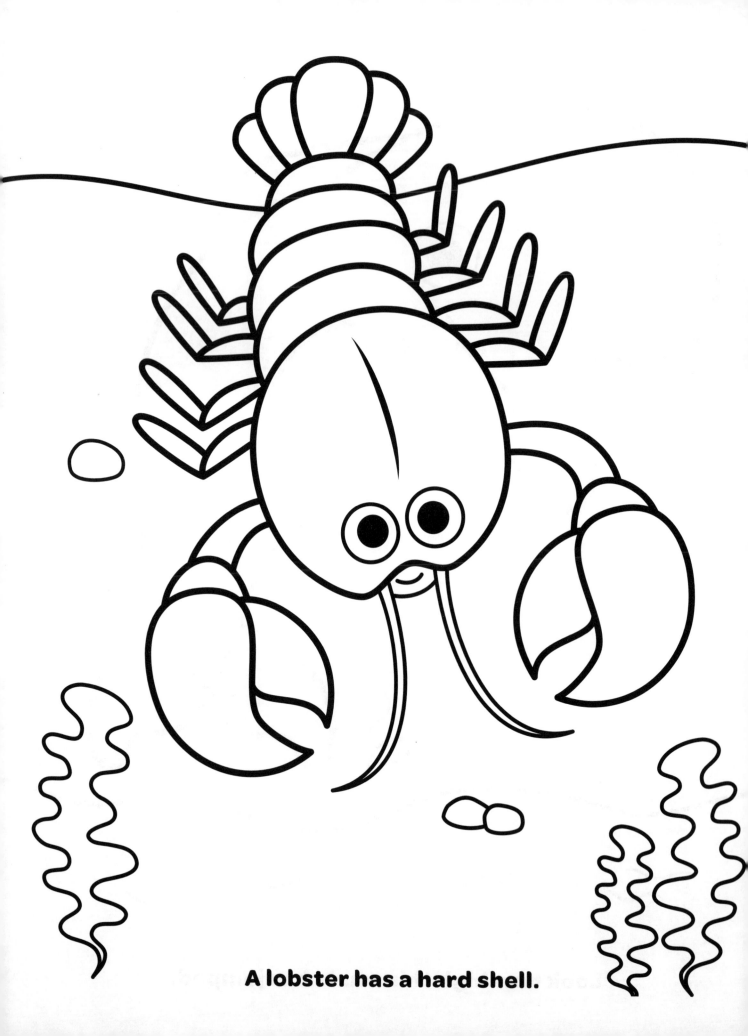

A lobster has a hard shell.

Thanks for visiting the ocean!

A giraffe has a long neck.

The teddy bear loves her magic wand.

Have a magical day!